ALIEN INVADERS

Don't miss any of the titles

in the ALIEN INVADERS series:

www.**kids**at**random**house.co.uk

ALIEN INVADERS: JUNKJET, THE FLYING MENACE
A RED FOX BOOK 978 1 849 41236 0

First published in Great Britain by Red Fox,
an imprint of Random House Children's Books
A Random House Group Company

This edition published 2012

1 3 5 7 9 10 8 6 4 2

Text and illustrations copyright © David Sinden,
Guy Macdonald and Matthew Morgan, 2012
Cover and interior illustrations, map and gaming cards by Dynamo Design
Designed by Nikalas Catlow

The right of David Sinden, Guy Macdonald and Matthew Morgan
to be identified as the authors of this work has been asserted in accordance
with the Copyright, Designs and Patents Act 1988.

The Random House Group Limited supports The Forest Stewardship
Council (FSC®), the leading international forest certification organisation.
Our books carrying the FSC label are printed on FSC® certified paper.
FSC is the only forest certification scheme endorsed by the leading
environmental organisations, including Greenpeace.
Our paper procurement policy can be found at
www.randomhouse.co.uk/environment

MIX
Paper from
responsible sources
FSC
www.fsc.org   FSC® C016897

Set in Century Schoolbook

Red Fox Books are published by
Random House Children's Books, 61–63 Uxbridge Road, London W5 5SA

www.kidsatrandomhouse.co.uk
www.randomhouse.co.uk

Addresses for companies within The Random House Group Limited can be
found at: www.randomhouse.co.uk/offices.htm

THE RANDOM HOUSE GROUP Limited Reg. No. 954009

A CIP catalogue record for this book is available from
the British Library.

Printed and bound by CPI Group (UK) Ltd, Croydon, CR0 4YY

ALIEN INVADERS

MAX SILVER

JUNKJET
THE FLYING MENACE

RED FOX

THE GALAXY

Cosmo's route - - - -

DELTA QUADRANT

GAMMA QUADRANT

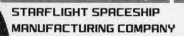

STARFLIGHT SPACESHIP
MANUFACTURING COMPANY

PLANET SYN-NOVA

PLANET BALAZ

SYSTEM OPEX

ALPHA QUADRANT

MOON OF GARR

GALACTIC CORE

BETA QUADRANT

THE WRECKING ZONE

PLANET KEFU

RESISTANCE IS FUTILE, EARTHLINGS!

MY NAME IS KAOS, AND MY WAR WITH YOUR GALAXY IS ENTERING A NEW PHASE...

THE YEAR IS 2121 AND I HAVE JOINED FORCES WITH METALLICON ALIENS FROM THE UNIVERSE'S WRECKING ZONE. THEY HAVE THE POWER OF LIVING MACHINES, AND I AM PROGRAMMING THEM TO INVADE YOUR GALAXY.

YOUR SECURITY FORCE, G-WATCH, WILL BE POWERLESS TO DEFEND YOU, AND ITS EARTHLING AGENT, COSMO SANTOS, WILL BE ANNIHILATED ALONG WITH HIS FRIENDS.

RESISTANCE IS FUTILE, EARTHLINGS. THE GALAXY WILL BE MINE!

INVADER ALERT!

In a glass-domed spaceship showroom in the Noverian Orb Fields, Frink Blatter pointed one of his hairy Ubliac arms to a sleek red racing ship. "Look, Dad, there's a Zephron!" he said excitedly.

Frink's dad frowned. "We're not buying a Zephron, Frink." He headed instead to a saucer-ship with a bubble cockpit in its centre. "How about this Moonbeam Reliable? I've heard it's very fuel-efficient."

Then he ran his hand along the fin of a white wagonship. "Or maybe a Roomstar?"

"Are they fast, Dad?" Frink asked.

"We don't need a fast spaceship, Frink. We need something practical." His dad gestured to a bald Riverian saleswoman in an orange spacesuit bearing the logo of the Starflight Spaceship Manufacturing Company. "Can I have some assistance here, please?" he asked.

As the saleswoman approached, Frink glanced over once more at the racing ships. "Can I just take a quick look at the Zephron, Dad? *Pleeease*."

"OK," his dad said. "But no touching."

"I won't!" Frink ran across the domed showroom, past microships and toolships, to the racing ships section. The Zephron looked even better up close: a single-seater arrowhead rocketship in racing red. He glanced back, checking that his dad and the saleswoman weren't watching, then climbed up into the cockpit and dropped into the pilot seat. The cockpit hood closed automatically over his head and he gripped the steering column. *Awesome!*

Frink looked up through the showroom's glass dome into space, pretending he was flying. But then he spotted an object flying down towards them. *Probably another customer,* he thought. *I'd better get out.* But the object was coming in too fast to be a customer in a spaceship. *Whoa! Way too fast!*

There came the sound of breaking glass as a massive machine smashed through the dome into the showroom. Frink buried his head in his hands, debris clattering against the Zephron's hull. He peered out at the wreckage: spaceships lay upturned and mangled, fragments of glass everywhere. *Dad*, Frink thought, concerned. In all the confusion, he couldn't see if his dad was safe.

Then he heard the roar of a jet engine and gasped as the machine rose from the showroom floor. It was some kind of freak alien, unlike anything he'd ever seen before: a huge living machine with wings and jets.

Time to get out of here, Frink thought, fumbling for the release switch to the cockpit hood. But in his panic, he hit the wrong one. The Zephron's control panel lit up and an electronic voice sounded. "Launch mode commencing . . ." The ship's nose tilted upwards. "Preparing for blast-off . . ." Frink gulped, not knowing what to do; he had never flown a spaceship before. "Have a safe flight," the electronic voice said as the Zephron's fins extended from its sides. Frink saw the freakish machine-like alien coming for him. As the Zephron's thrusters ignited, the alien swiped a large metal claw, striking it with a *CLANG!*

"I am Junkjet!" the alien roared. "And I'm here to tear this place apart!"

CHAPTER ONE

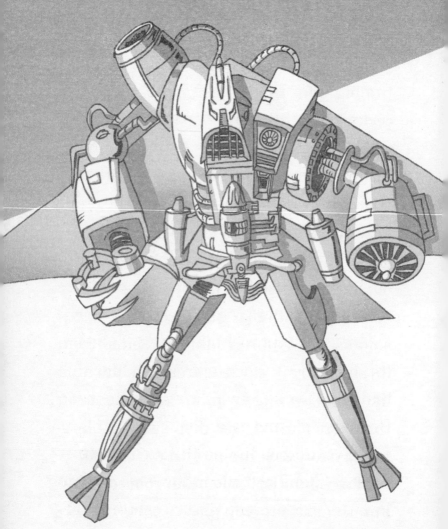

COLLISION COURSE

"Look at me! I'm flying, Master Cosmo!"

Cosmo chuckled as the ship's brainbot, Brain-E, came whizzing through the Dragster 7000's cockpit, wearing a new copter-blade attachment that it had found on the kit shelf. "Way to go, Brain-E!" Cosmo said.

The brainbot circled the navigation console, then tried a loop-the-loop, crashing into the spacescreen and ricocheting off

the steering column. It landed with a
bump! on the control desk. "Oops!"

"Don't worry, Brain-E, you'll soon get
the hang of it," Cosmo said encouragingly.

"I hope so. This could come in handy
on our mission, Master Cosmo."

Cosmo smiled, glad to have Brain-E
with him.

"Look sharp, you two. In ten seconds
we exit hyperdrive," interrupted Agent
Nuri, Cosmo's Etrusian co-pilot. She
quickly unscrewed Brain-E's copter

attachment and Cosmo took the Dragster's controls, counting down in his head. *Ten . . . nine . . . eight . . .*

They were blasting along Hyperway 62 on a dangerous mission for the galactic security force, G-Watch. Five alien invaders were being beamed into the galaxy by the evil outlaw Kaos, and it was down to Cosmo and his team to stop them. The invaders were metallicons, android aliens from a distant spacedump known as the Wrecking Zone, and had been programmed by Kaos with orders to destroy. Cosmo had already defeated the first of them: Krush, the iron giant, and was now speeding to the galaxy's Delta Quadrant to fight the second invader: Junkjet. G-Watch scanners had identified the alien beaming towards the headquarters of the Starflight Spaceship Manufacturing Company.

. . . three . . . two . . . one . . . Cosmo flicked a silver switch then turned the

steering column, feeling his ears pop as the spaceship veered off the hyperway. He slowed to seven vectrons, and stars reappeared in the spacescreen. Directly ahead he saw a cluster of shining planets with siphon ships docked alongside.

"Those planets are called the Noverian Orbs," Nuri said. "The Starflight Company uses them."

"Uses them? For what?"

"To build spaceships from. They're planets of molten metal from which raw materials are extracted by siphon ship."

On the spacescreen a message flashed up: STARFLIGHT TERRITORY – ACCESS RESTRICTED.

"Access restricted – how come?" Cosmo asked.

Brain-E bleeped from the control desk.

"The Starflight Spaceship Manufacturing Company occupies this whole region. There is an open-access spaceway to its public showroom but all other areas are off-limits on account of its hazardous test zone and top-secret factory. Starflight is one of the galaxy's largest companies, building millions of spaceships every year."

"And G-Watch scanners picked up Junkjet heading this way," Cosmo replied, concerned. "OK, Brain-E, what do we know about this alien invader?"

The brainbot's lights flashed as it searched its databank for information. "G-Watch reconnaissance probes from the Wrecking Zone record this alien as a winged assassin capable of tearing to pieces any vessel in its path."

"Well, if Junkjet tries anything with us, we'll send him back to his junkyard!" Cosmo said defiantly. His courage grew and his spacesuit began to glow.

Cosmo was wearing the Quantum Mutation Suit, a living body armour which allowed him to mutate into awesome alien forms. It was activated by the power of the universe – a power present in all living things, but uniquely strong in Cosmo.

"Get ready," Nuri said, checking the navigation console. "Junkjet will have beamed in somewhere around here."

Cosmo reduced power to the thrusters as he flew past another orb attended by Starflight siphon ships. Suddenly a light flashed on the communications console indicating an incoming message.

"It's an open frequency broadcast from another spaceship," Nuri said, flicking a switch to open the channel.

"Help! Somebody help me!" shouted a panicked voice over the airwaves. "I can't fly this thing!"

It sounds like a boy's voice, Cosmo thought. "Send a reply, Nuri," he said.

Nuri connected to the frequency. "This is G-Watch in the Dragster 7000. Please state your name and location."

"My name's Frink Blatter," a voice replied. "And I'm aaar—"

"Spaceship incoming, Master Cosmo," Brain-E interrupted, pointing its metal arm to the Dragster's radar. A light on the display indicated a spaceship coming straight towards them at high speed.

Cosmo quickly turned the steering column to avoid a collision as a Zephron racing ship appeared and shot past like a dart, speeding towards one of the molten metal orbs where the siphon ships were at work. Cosmo gasped. "It's out of control!"

Brain-E's lights flashed as it ran diagnostics. "And on a course to collide with that orb in precisely seventy-six Earth seconds."

Cosmo banked the Dragster and increased speed, racing after the Zephron.

"Frink, this is Agent Cosmo Santos in the Dragster 7000," he radioed. "I'm coming after you. Steer away from those orbs."

"There's something wrong with this thing's steering," Frink replied. "And I don't know how to slow down!"

Flying at high speed, Cosmo brought the Dragster closer to the Zephron.

"One of its thrusters is damaged and the hull's badly ripped," Nuri said, peering through the spacescreen. "I can see broken cabling too."

Cosmo glimpsed a hairy Ubliac boy in the Zephron's cockpit, his arms trembling as he tried to fly the stricken spaceship.

"Frink, you've got to reduce speed now and change course or you're going to collide with that orb straight ahead," Cosmo instructed over the communicator.

"I'm trying, but the steering column won't budge," the boy replied, panic rising in his voice.

Nuri turned to Cosmo. "The damage to the Zephron's cabling could have jammed its controls," she told him.

The racing ship was hurtling closer to the molten metal planet.

"Direct impact in forty-nine seconds," Brain-E said.

"Help!" Frink yelled over the airwaves.

"OK, Nuri, take the controls," Cosmo told his co-pilot, unbuckling his flying harness and leaving his seat. "Fly us directly above the Zephron. I'm going to try and pull Frink out of there."

"At this speed? Are you crazy?"

"We have no choice. In about forty seconds the Zephron will hit that orb and explode, and Frink and any workers on those siphon ships will go up in a fireball." Cosmo swallowed an oxygen pill, then closed his helmet's visor.

"Thirty-eight seconds now, Master Cosmo," Brain-E said.

Cosmo quickly dropped into the Dragster's airlock and closed the hatch behind him. He attached himself to the space-walk harness, checking its safety cable was firmly secured to the Dragster, then he opened the airlock's external

hatch. They were flying directly above the Zephron.

"That's it, Nuri, hold us steady," he said into his helmet mic. He focused, summoning the power inside him, then took a deep breath and jumped.

CHAPTER TWO

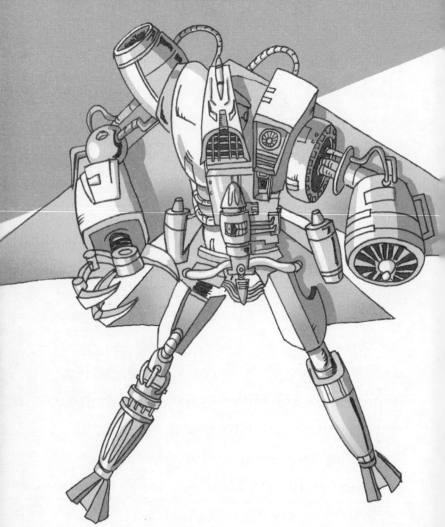

UNDETECTABLE

The safety cable to Cosmo's space-walk harness stretched out as he threw himself at the speeding Zephron. He landed with a thud, got hold of its fin, then began pulling himself along the ship's hull. He squinted in the silver glare of the molten metal orb ahead, which was growing brighter and larger by the second.

"Cosmo, hurry! Time's running out," he heard Nuri say over his earpiece.

Cosmo clambered along to the Zephron's cockpit hood and pulled a lever on its side. The hood flew up and he reached in, passing the Ubliac boy an oxygen pill. "Swallow this," he said.

Frink did as instructed and Cosmo gripped him firmly under his arms, then called into his communicator, "I've got him, Nuri! Get us out of here now!"

The Dragster suddenly decelerated and Cosmo was yanked off the Zephron by the safety cable, with Frink in his arms. "Whoooaa!" They swung on the cable beneath the Dragster's open airlock as the Zephron sped away from them towards the metal orb.

Cosmo called into his mic, "Nuri, we're out. Destroy the Zephron NOW before it hits the siphon ships and the orb."

The Dragster's cannons engaged, firing a volley of photon torpedoes towards the racing ship, blasting it to pieces.

"Impact averted," he heard Brain-E
say through his earpiece.

"Nice shooting, Nuri. Bring us in."

The Dragster banked away from the
explosion, then the safety cable retracted,
reeling Frink and Cosmo back into the

airlock. Reaching safety, Cosmo closed the outer hatch behind them, the airlock pressurized and Frink gasped with relief.

"Thank you! You saved my life," he said.

"No problem. But what were you doing in that Zephron if you don't know how to fly it?" Cosmo asked, opening the hatch and pulling himself back into the cockpit.

"I only meant to sit in it and pretend," the boy replied. "I was in the Starflight showroom with my dad. An enormous alien attacked and I panicked, trying to get out of there."

"An enormous alien attacked the Starflight showroom?"

"Yes, and my dad's still in there!"

Cosmo exchanged a concerned glance with Nuri. "Junkjet," he said. "Nuri, set a course for the Starflight showroom, fast."

"I'm on to it." Nuri powered the Dragster up to full speed, heading for a floating domed structure marked on the star plotter. As they approached, Cosmo saw that its glass dome was shattered, with a large chunk missing. Starflight emergency droneships had arrived and were spraying gravity enhancer at it to stop the whole place breaking up and floating away.

Nuri flew the Dragster inside. "It looks like a bomb's hit this place," she said, landing the craft amongst the debris of destroyed spaceships.

Cosmo looked for Junkjet, but couldn't see him anywhere. "Stay alert, team." He opened the cockpit's door and jumped down into the showroom, his boots scrunching on broken glass. He noticed spaceships with their wings ripped off and hulls torn open, engine parts hanging out.

The boy, Frink, hurried to a group of Starflight emergency droids who were helping an Ubliac man and a bald Riverian saleswoman to their feet. "Dad!" he cried.

"Frink, you're alive!" the Ubliac man called with relief, reaching out to hug his son.

"Is everyone OK?" Cosmo asked, going over to speak to them.

"I will be in a moment, thank you," the saleswoman replied shakily.

"What happened here exactly?"

"An alien smashed into the showroom," Frink's dad said. "He went berserk, tearing spaceships apart."

"And then what?" Cosmo asked, wondering where Junkjet had got to.

"That was the strangest thing: one second he was ripping the ships apart, and the next he vanished."

"Vanished?" Cosmo asked curiously.

"Cosmo, quick, come and look at this," Nuri called from across the showroom.

Cosmo hurried to her. "What have you found?"

Nuri was clambering over the wreckage of a large hexagonal ship. "This is a K57 Scorpion, a reconnaissance craft built for observing new species in wild space. It uses a cloaking device that acts like a virtual mirror, making it undetectable."

"So?"

"Its cloaking device has been taken!"

Brain-E dipped its probe arm into a drop of silver slime on the smashed hull of the spacecraft. "I'm detecting traces of metallicon protein here," it said. "Metallicon aliens are capable of absorbing other technologies and using them as their own. It's my guess that Junkjet took the cloaking device and assimilated it into his body."

"You mean he's using it like a spaceship would? No wonder he suddenly vanished; he'll be invisible now!" Cosmo suddenly looked around, worried in case Junkjet was still nearby.

"If he was still here, Cosmo, he'd have attacked us by now," Nuri said.

"So where is he? And what's he up to?"

"Brain-E, if you were an alien invading this area, is there another target you might be after?" Nuri asked. "A bigger one?"

The brainbot bleeped, searching its databank. "The Starflight spaceship factory," it responded. "It's the hub of all Starflight's manufacturing operations."

"Then we should head there straight away," Cosmo said. He called to Frink, "We've got to go now. Nice meeting you. Stay safe." Then he raced back to the Dragster. "Nuri, Brain-E, we have to stop Junkjet before he reaches the Starflight factory!"

CHAPTER THREE

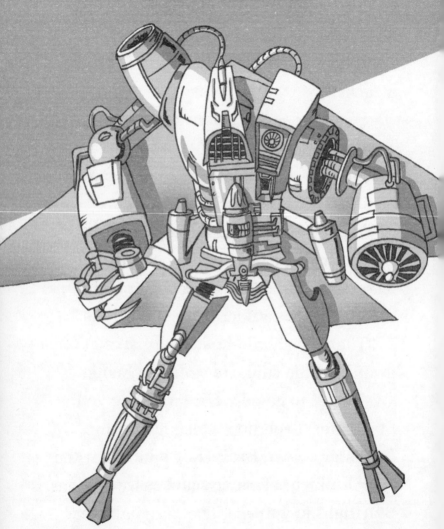

INTO THE TEST ZONE

Cosmo blasted the Dragster away from the showroom in pursuit of Junkjet. "Which way to the Starflight factory, Nuri?"

"Adjust course forty degrees east," Nuri replied, checking the navigation console. "It's beyond the test zone."

Cosmo turned the steering column, approaching a vast area of space marked by flashing beacons, rigs and space stations.

Brain-E bleeped. "The Starflight test

zone is a hazardous place to fly, Master. It's where prototype vessels are flight-tested before going into production. These rigs and space stations simulate dangerous conditions that they may encounter. It will be safer to navigate around it to reach the factory even though the route is longer."

"We've no time for that," Cosmo said. He patted the Dragster's control desk and smiled. "I think G-Watch's most advanced spaceship can handle a few flight tests, Brain-E." And he flew into the test zone through a line of space beacons.

He noticed some of the beacons were mangled, their lights smashed out. "I reckon Junkjet's come through this way too, Nuri," he said. "We should warn any ships in the area to get away."

"I'll send out a call," Nuri replied, switching on the communicator. "G-Watch calling all pilots in the test zone. We have an emergency. All ships to leave at once."

But from the Dragster's communicator came only the crackling sound of static.

"Calling all test pilots," Nuri repeated.

Brain-E's lights flashed. "Some kind of digital interference appears to be present," it said. "Try the radar."

Nuri switched on the radar screen, but that was fuzzy from interference too.

"Junkjet must be transmitting a swamping signal to hamper communications," Brain-E said.

But then Nuri leaned closer to the ship's communicator, her ultra-sensitive Etrusian ears twitching as she listened. "I'm detecting a faint signal from the upper test zone," she said.

Nuri's hearing could outsmart any swamping signal, and sure enough, when she amplified the background sounds, Cosmo could just make out a faint sequence of beeps behind the static: three short, three long, three short. "It's an SOS distress signal from a spaceship!" he realized. "I bet Junkjet's there. Hold onto your seats!"

Cosmo powered the Dragster onwards between large spinning rigs that acted as wind generators. The ship rolled as the winds hit, sending Brain-E somersaulting.

"We're flying through an artificial tornado for testing stormcraft," the brainbot cried, tumbling across the control desk.

"No problem," Cosmo replied, flicking a green switch. "Engaging auxiliary wings." Slits opened along the Dragster's hull and six smaller wings pushed outwards, each with a rocket at its tip. "Blasting us back on course!"

Cosmo pressed a button, igniting the rockets, and the Dragster accelerated and stabilized. With thrust coming from all sides and extra wing surfaces to hold the ship level, it cut through the tornado, powering on past the wind generators.

"Adjust route by three degrees north," Nuri said, checking the navigation console.

Cosmo flicked the green switch again, this time to retract the auxiliary wings, then veered north towards what looked like flickering red lights in the distance. They grew larger as he approached.

"Artificial fire-stars," Brain-E said. "Be careful, Master. They'll be scorching hot."

Each star was a huge burning ball of fire emitting immense heat. Cosmo held his course, shooting between them, and the Dragster's spacescreen glowed red.

Brain-E hopped, its tiny metal feet heating up as the control desk warmed beneath them. "Oo! Ow! I don't like this!"

Cosmo shielded his eyes, feeling the colossal heat through the spacescreen.

"The fire-stars provide a heat test for solar ships, Master Cosmo!"

"Engaging heat shields," Cosmo said, pressing a line of buttons to his right. With a series of clangs, black tinted scales crystallized over the exterior of the Dragster, encasing the ship like armour, forming a barrier to the heat. Instantly the cockpit temperature cooled.

"That's better," Nuri said, wiping sweat from her face.

"Good work, Master Cosmo," Brain-E said, shaking its feet to cool them.

"No problem," Cosmo replied, smiling. He powered the Dragster beyond the fire-stars, then disengaged the heat shields. The SOS distress signal was still sounding over the crackling communicator as they neared the upper test zone.

The spaceship shot between large weather stations that were pumping out a gloopy green substance.

"What is this stuff, Brain-E?" Cosmo asked.

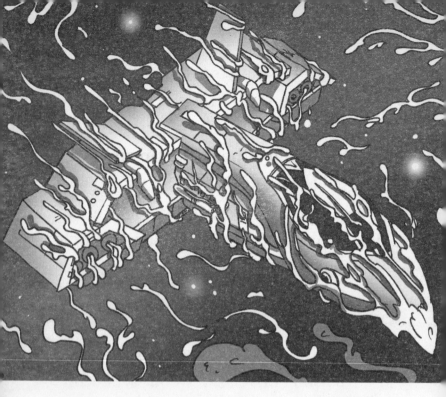

"Simulated nebulae weed, a substance encountered when glutinous planets explode," Brain-E explained.

Nuri giggled. "Also known as space snot."

Strands of it clung to the Dragster's spacescreen, then tangled round its wings and thrusters. The ship shuddered and warning lights flashed on the control desk as the engines started to clog.

"Engaging suction hoses," Cosmo said,

reaching for two small joysticks on the side of the control desk. As he nudged them, two external cleaning hoses extended from either wing tip and slid into the thrusters, hosing them clean.

The Dragster emerged from the nebulae weed, and Cosmo saw a mangled Starflight satellite ahead. "Junkjet's been here all right," he said. They shot past it, heading towards what looked like shining ice mountains floating in space.

"Spacebergs, Master," Brain-E warned.

Cosmo slowed to two vectrons, steering the Dragster cautiously between them. They looked enormous and foreboding, casting huge shadows over the ship.

"Carefully does it," Nuri said.

Cosmo turned on the ship's searchlights and their beams flickered eerily on the ice. All around he could hear creaking sounds and the dull booms of spacebergs colliding. One scraped against the Dragster's hull, sending shivers down his spine; another floated into view directly ahead. Cosmo gasped as he saw a large armoured ship wedged into the ice. "I think we've found where that SOS distress signal has been coming from," he said, pointing to it.

"That would appear to be a Polark spaceberg melter, Master Cosmo," Brain-E said. "It must be being tested here."

"But it's stuck!" Nuri said.

"It's more than stuck, Nuri," Cosmo added, flying nearer. He could make out gouges in the hull where it had been ripped open, and smoke rising up the edge of the spaceberg, colouring it black. "Junkjet's attacked it!" he exclaimed. "Nuri, take the controls." Cosmo unfastened his flying harness and found a jetpack on the kit shelf. "I'm going to check the pilot's OK."

He jumped into the airlock, then heard Nuri's voice in his earpiece. "Just take care out there, Cosmo," she told him. "Junkjet could still be nearby."

CHAPTER FOUR

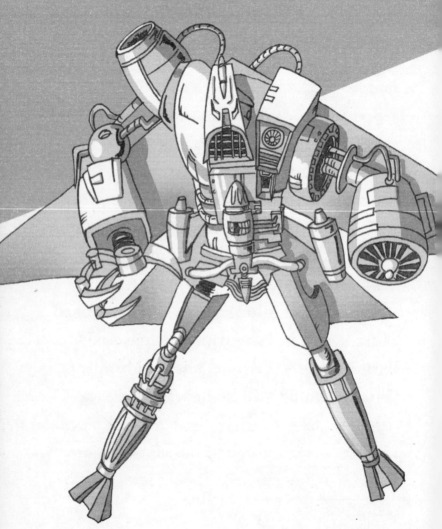

FIRE IN THE HOLD

Cosmo leaped out of the airlock into the zero gravity of space. Frost formed on his Quantum Mutation Suit as he floated weightlessly among the icy spacebergs, but the suit's hi-tech membrane kept him warm. He pressed the buttons on the jetpack's joysticks, igniting the jets and propelling himself past broken chunks of ice towards the stricken Polark ship.

Its cockpit was wedged in the ice, so Cosmo headed for a hole ripped in the ship's hull. He pulled himself inside and peered along a corridor, which was filling with smoke. "Anyone still on board?" he called. But his voice was muffled by his helmet.

He looked for the pilot, but found the cockpit empty, with the ship's communicator flashing, transmitting the SOS signal they'd picked up in the Dragster.

As Cosmo jetted back into the smoke-filled corridor to check the rear of the ship, he heard Brain-E's voice over his earpiece. "Master Cosmo, if the fire reaches the fuel bay, the whole vessel will blow. Hurry out of there."

"Copy that, Brain-E," Cosmo replied. He yanked open the metal door to the hold, and smoke billowed out. Inside, flames were spewing from the wall

cavities, vents and shafts. The helmeted
figure of a hawk-headed test pilot stood
with a flame-freezer in his hands, trying
to put out the fire.

"You've got to get out of here!" Cosmo
called, grabbing hold of him. "The ship's
going to blow at any second!"

He dragged the pilot out and pulled him
along the smoke-filled corridor, heading
towards the hole in the ship's hull.

Suddenly there came a *BOOM!* as the fire reached the Polark's fuel tanks and the ship exploded, sending Cosmo and the test pilot tumbling head over heels into space.

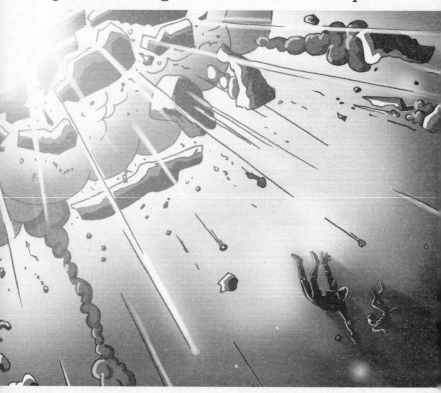

Cosmo reached for the pilot with one hand and, with the other, fired his jetpack to steady himself. He glanced back and saw only chunks of debris where the Polark had been. Then he jetted back to the Dragster with the pilot in his grasp, and pulled him into the safety of the airlock.

Once it had pressurized, Cosmo led the pilot up into the cockpit and laid him on the Dragster's rest bunk. "You can lie down here to recover," he told him.

The pilot removed his helmet, then gasped with relief. "Thank you."

"Are you OK?" Nuri asked from the co-pilot's seat.

"I am now," the pilot said, brushing soot from his spacesuit. "Who are you guys anyway? Those aren't Starflight uniforms."

"We're from G-Watch," Cosmo told him, taking off his jetpack. "My name's Cosmo Santos and this is my co-pilot, Agent Nuri. What happened to your ship?"

"I was in the middle of a berg-melting test, everything going fine, when suddenly the ship started shaking," the pilot replied. "I thought I'd hit a patch of space frost but couldn't see any warning on the ship's sensors."

Cosmo and Nuri looked at one another anxiously.

"Before I knew what was going on, I felt the Polark being hurled into that spaceberg. The hull was torn open, then the ship's thermal blaster was ripped off."

"Thermal blaster?"

"It's like a huge flame-thrower which the Polark uses to melt spacebergs. It suddenly vanished, then flames appeared as if from nowhere, setting fire to the ship."

"Nuri, Brain-E, it sounds like Junkjet's stolen a thermal blaster now, as well as a cloaking device," Cosmo said.

"A cloaking device? Was I attacked by something invisible?" the pilot asked, bewildered.

"By an alien invader – a techno freak called Junkjet," Cosmo replied, getting back into his seat. "He has a cloaking device to hide himself, but he can't be far ahead of us."

As Cosmo blasted the Dragster onwards, the pilot tugged at his arm. "The Polark isn't the only ship in the test zone. My buddy's testing a Vorp-X comet clearer in the comet lane up ahead. I tried radioing him for help, but couldn't get a signal."

"A Vorp-X comet clearer?" Cosmo asked anxiously. "Does it have any special technologies that Mister Invisible might want to steal?"

"It's testing a prototype gamma vaporizer for disintegrating comets."

"A gamma vaporizer! That's deadly!" Nuri exclaimed. "Cosmo, full speed ahead to the comet lane. We've got to find that Vorp-X before Junkjet does."

CHAPTER FIVE

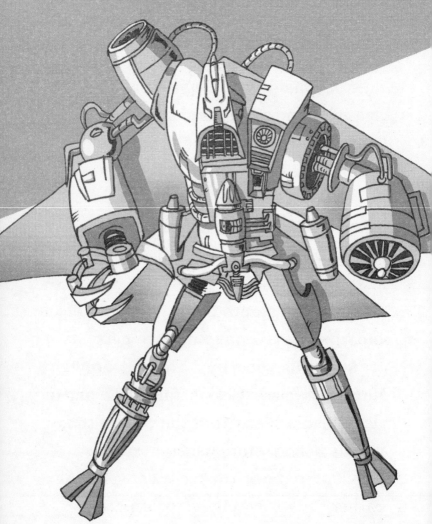

BAM! BAM! BAM!

The Dragster left the spacebergs behind and sped onwards, seeking out the comet lane. Cosmo spotted the comets far ahead: hundreds of them circling, their streaking trails lighting the darkness of space like interlinking coloured rings. As the Dragster flew closer, he saw that the comets were orbiting space stations mounted with gravity enhancers to keep them circling rather than shooting off into space.

Brain-E bleeped nervously. "Master Cosmo, I would advise extreme caution," it said. "If a single comet collides with the Dragster, we'll be smashed to pieces."

"The robot's right," the pilot from the Polark added. "Only a comet clearer could get through this lot, by blasting a path with its vaporizer."

Cosmo looked for the Vorp-X comet clearer and spotted it amongst the comets, its hull torn open. "Junkjet's got to the Vorp-X already by the looks of it," he said. "It needs help. Hold on tight. We're going in."

Cosmo powered up the Dragster's thrusters and sped between flashing space beacons. Red and blue comets streaked past, debris and dust from their trails clattering against the spacescreen. "Engaging photon cannons. It's time to do some comet clearing of our own," he said, flicking a switch on the steering column.

An electronic display appeared on the spacescreen with a cross-target in its centre. As a comet flew into range he let off a round of photon torpedoes.

BAM! The comet exploded in a burst of heat and light. *BAM! BAM!* He blasted another two, creating a path to the Vorp-X.

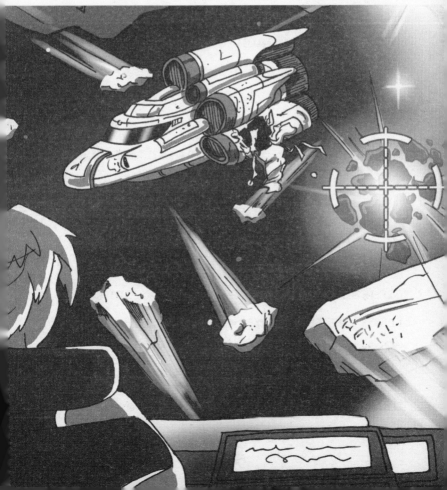

"Its cabling's hanging out," Nuri said.

Brain-E bleeped. "Oh dear, by the looks of things its gamma vaporizer has been ripped off. It's defenceless."

Cosmo could see the Vorp-X's pilot at the controls, trying to steer the stricken ship between the incoming comets, but without its vaporizer to clear a path through, it was being pummelled from all sides.

"Let's get it out of here," Cosmo said, flying alongside the Vorp-X and signalling the pilot to follow the Dragster.

The pilot saluted from his cockpit, and Cosmo flew ahead, protecting the Vorp-X by blasting comets out of the way with photon torpedoes. The comet clearer followed close behind, using the Dragster as a shield.

When they emerged into open space, Cosmo breathed a sigh of relief.

The hawk-headed pilot he'd saved from the Polark waved to his friend in the Vorp-X, relieved he was safe. "Nice flying, Cosmo Santos," he said. "Have you ever thought of becoming a test pilot?"

Cosmo smiled. "Maybe one day," he replied. "But right now I've got an alien invader to fight – an invisible invader armed with a thermal blaster and now a gamma vaporizer."

He tapped the spacescreen, activating its star plotter, and the words STARFLIGHT FACTORY lit up on the glass, marking an astral object in the distance. Cosmo turned to the Polark pilot. "I'll need to transfer you from here to the Vorp-X. Tell its pilot to keep away from the factory though – it's too dangerous. We believe Junkjet is heading that way: we're going to try to stop him before he turns the Starflight factory into a wrecking zone of his own."

CHAPTER SIX

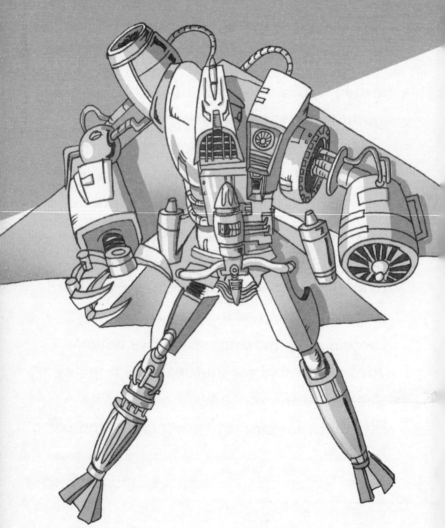

"VICTORY IS OURS!"

Far beyond the galaxy, on the battleship *Oblivion*, the five-headed outlaw Kaos stared through a porthole at the floating junk of the Wrecking Zone: rusted hulls of old spaceships, destroyed machinery and barrels of toxic waste adrift in space. "What a dump," Kaos's first head groaned. "The sooner we get out of here, the better."

"Before long we'll return to the galaxy, triumphant," his second head replied.

"When Junkjet destroys Starflight, the galaxy's supply of spaceships will come to a halt. Galactic civilization will crumble and G-Watch will beg for mercy!"

"Well, let's see if your plan is working," Kaos's third head said. It glanced at a purple rat scurrying along a bank of digital monitors. "Wugrat, what's the news of Junkjet's invasion?"

"*Eeek*," the rat squeaked, pointing its paw at electronic graphs and scanners showing the metallicon's vital functions.

Kaos came over. "See how strong Junkjet is," his second head said proudly.

"*Eek, eek!*" Wugrat squeaked nervously.

"Don't fret, Wugrat. The Earthling boy is no match for *this* metallicon. Junkjet will tear him to pieces. Tune in to the live video from Junkjet's optical nerves."

Wugrat scratched at buttons on the monitors, and images appeared of a dented Vorp-X comet clearer and G-Watch's Dragster 7000 emerging from the Starflight test zone. Kaos watched intently as a test pilot transferred from the Dragster to the comet clearer by jetpack. Then the Dragster sped away and, as it did so, the camera followed, Junkjet setting off in pursuit.

Kaos's five heads grinned.

"Ha-ha! Junkjet is using the cloaking device as I instructed," his second head gloated. "G-Watch think they're following him, when in fact *they're* now being followed. It's only a matter of time before they are dead and victory is ours!"

"The Starflight factory should be coming into view now," Nuri said, checking the navigation console on the Dragster's control desk.

Cosmo stared out at a distant floating platform dotted with lights, machinery and buildings. He approached, fearful of what wreckage he might find, but saw that the factory was still intact and fully

operational. Spaceships were being assembled robotically in docking bays and on launch pads, and operating cranes were lifting machine parts. Hangars stood open with newly-built ships lined up: space shuttles, interstellar explorers, drop-ships, rocketships, labships and waste barges. "Junkjet hasn't struck yet," Cosmo said, relieved.

"But this *has* to be his main target,"

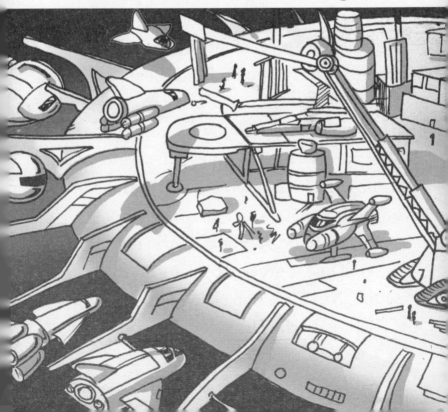

Nuri said. "And if he's using the cloaking device, he could be around here now, getting ready to attack."

Cosmo had an idea. He turned a dial on the control desk, amplifying the external gauges. "We may not be able to *see* Junkjet, but we might just be able to *listen* for him," he said. Sounds came over the loudspeaker from outside the spaceship: the ambient hum of space . . . the distant machinery from the factory . . . and the low throb of jet engines. "Those engines aren't coming from the direction of the factory, they're coming from behind us," Cosmo said, quickly turning the Dragster round and staring fearfully out through the spacescreen. He couldn't see any ships though.

"It has to be Junkjet!" Nuri said.

"Give me a precise bearing on that sound, Nuri," Cosmo asked her.

Suddenly the Dragster shook violently

and a jet of flames blasted its spacescreen. The cockpit siren sounded: *Whoop! Whoop!*

"We're under attack!" Cosmo yelled. Increasing power to the thrusters, he veered left, trying to evade the invisible attacker. "Engaging emergency force field!" he said, flicking a switch on the control desk. An electric blue membrane radiated from the ship.

More flames came at them from the left, then from the right, and muffled booms sounded as the Dragster's force field deflected the hits.

"Master, the Dragster's force field won't hold out for ever," Brain-E said.

"Then it's time to give Junkjet a taste of his own medicine." Cosmo flicked the safety cap from the thumb trigger on his steering column, engaging the photon cannons. As a fiery jet blasted the Dragster, Cosmo launched a photon torpedo back towards its source. But with the alien invisible, it missed. "He's dodging and I can't see him!" Cosmo said, frustrated, firing again.

Suddenly there came a blinding flash of red light and the Dragster rocked violently.

"What was that?" Cosmo asked.

"Junkjet's attacking us with the gamma vaporizer that he stole from the Vorp-X," Nuri said.

There came another flash, and the

Dragster shuddered again. Warning lights flashed on the control desk, and the blue force field surrounding the ship dimmed.

"The force field's been breached!" Brain-E cried.

From the Dragster's hull came a *thud!* as if something had landed on it. It was followed by the sound of scraping metal, and gashes appeared in the portside fin. A panel peeled away from the nose-cone.

"Junkjet's on the Dragster! He's tearing it apart!" Nuri peered out through the spacescreen as cables started spilling out.

Cosmo turned the steering column sharply, trying to throw the invisible invader off. But Junkjet held firm.

Next they heard a clang on the underside of the hull, followed by the sound of more tearing metal. A light flashed on the control desk, indicating a malfunction to the spaceship's weapons system.

"He's stealing the Dragster's photon cannons!" Cosmo exclaimed. Then the spacescreen shuddered as if the invader was trying to smash his way inside. "Brain-E! Any bright ideas?"

Brain-E's lights flashed. "The force field's down but not completely out, Master Cosmo. If we redirect all available power to it, we might just give Junkjet a shock and shake him off."

"Are you crazy, Brain-E?" Nuri cried.

"Redirecting all power to the force field will stall the ship's engines. We'll be stranded!"

The spacescreen shuddered once more as the invisible invader tried to smash it in.

"It's our only chance!" Cosmo yelled. "Powering down now!" He flicked every switch on the control desk to OFF, and the engines were silent. "All power to the force field!" he said, pushing an overhead lever to MAX.

As the force field suddenly recharged, there was a dazzling flash of electric blue light outside followed by a hideous roar. The power surge had sent a shock through Junkjet, disabling his cloaking device, and the metallicon began materializing, firstly as silver specks, then in his terrifying solid form, directly in front of the spacescreen.

The invader had a huge metallic body with wings like a spacecraft and roaring jet engines. Mounted on his metal torso were weapons: the thermal blaster, the

gamma vaporizer and the Dragster's
photon cannons. He looked at the
spacescreen with angry red eyes.

"DESTROY!" he roared, pointing both
photon cannons straight at the Dragster.
He fired, and two torpedoes of blinding
white light blasted the ship's hull,

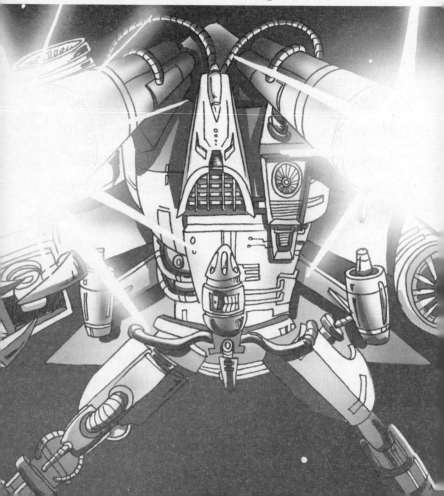

knocking out the fragile force field and sending the spaceship spinning.

Cosmo fought with the steering column, trying to regain control, but the Dragster was spiralling away, its power down. "Nuri, take over and try to stabilize us. Brain-E, see if you can access any power from the auxiliary cells." Cosmo left his seat and leaped into the airlock.

"What are you going to do, Cosmo?" Nuri asked.

"I'm going to deal with Junkjet." He closed the hatch after him, then opened the outer hatch and pushed himself out into space. He saw Junkjet powering away towards the factory, flames surging from his jet engines.

"Cosmo, you forgot your jetpack!" Nuri called over his earpiece.

"I won't be needing it," Cosmo replied into his helmet's mic. It was time to use the Quantum Mutation Suit and mutate!

CHAPTER SEVEN

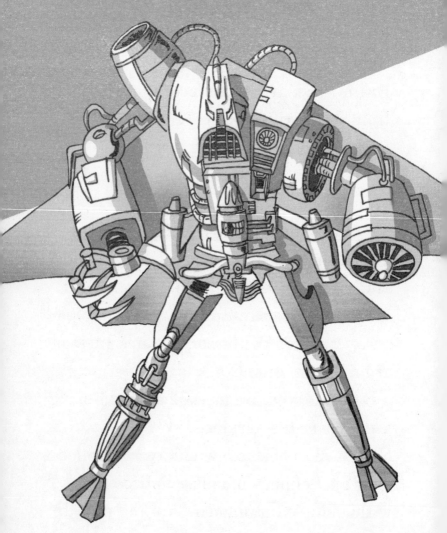

AERIAL COMBAT

"SCAN!" Cosmo said into the helmet of his Quantum Mutation Suit.

On the electronic visor in front of his eyes, images of alien creatures appeared as the suit scrolled through its databank: a spitting choku . . . a pike-finned dinol . . . a scissor-clawed gruke . . . *What alien can beat Junkjet?* Cosmo wondered. He spotted an image of a six-winged alien with a single large horn.

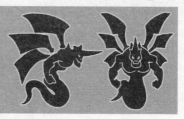

ALIEN: FRACTURAX
SPECIES: GORE-DACTYL
ORIGIN: PLANET COMROX
HEIGHT: 5 METRES
WEIGHT: 1 TONNE
FEATURE: DUELLING HORN

Fracturax's duelling horn will open Junkjet like a tin can! Cosmo thought, and he spoke the command: "MUTATE!"

Power surged through his body and the Quantum Mutation Suit glowed. He felt it meshing with his skin, his body tingling as the molecules inside him began to mutate into those of Fracturax. He grew larger, a hard pointed horn pushing out of his forehead, three pairs of wings sprouting from his back. Purple scales encased his body and his legs fused into a long swishy tail. Fracturax was ready to do battle! Cosmo beat his six wings and powered towards Junkjet like a missile.

The invader opened fire on the factory, shooting photon torpedoes at spaceships on the factory's assembly dock and

spewing jets of flames from the thermal
torch, melting factory robots.

"Hey, take this, *Punk*jet!" Cosmo roared,
about to strike with his duelling horn.

The invader spun round, surprised, as Cosmo pierced his metal flesh – *WHACK!*
The force of the collision sent the metallicon spinning.

"You've met your match now!" Cosmo called. Across the blackness of space, he saw Junkjet's eye-lights glaring at him.

"You won't beat me!" the invader snarled.

Cosmo dived towards him again, and Junkjet let rip with his gamma vaporizer, shooting streaks of burning red light.

But as Fracturax, Cosmo was a nimble flyer. With slight movements of his six wings, he swerved to avoid the deadly gamma rays.

BOOM! He struck Junkjet with his horn a second time, splitting panels on the invader's metal body and sheering off one of his fins. The alien tumbled backwards, and Cosmo circled to face him again, ready for the next charge.

Junkjet eyed him furiously. "Do not strike me again, freak!"

"CHARGE!" Cosmo cried defiantly. He beat his six wings and once again launched an aerial attack.

But this time, Junkjet chose to take Cosmo head on, flying directly towards him.

The two mighty aliens both accelerated towards one another on a collision course.

"Back down or I'll smash you to pieces!" Cosmo yelled.

"NEVER!" the alien roared, letting rip a volley of photon torpedoes.

Cosmo dipped and weaved, trying to avoid the deadly missiles of white light. But as he lowered his horn, ready to strike again, a torpedo smashed into his wing and his body crumpled. *I've been hit!* he realized.

"Ha! Now leave!" Junkjet roared, striking Cosmo with his metal claw as he whooshed past.

Down Cosmo fell, spinning towards the factory. He landed in a heap on one of its platforms, his alien form broken.

He could feel his power waning, and
Fracturax's molecular pattern started
breaking up. "RESET," he said.

Fracturax's six wings receded, his
tail split into two human legs, and his
injuries healed as he transformed back
into Cosmo's boy self.

Cosmo heard a screech of scraping

metal and turned to see the Dragster crash-land on the factory platform. It slid to a halt and Nuri leaped out and hurried towards him.

"Cosmo, are you OK?" she called.

"I don't think I can beat Junkjet in aerial combat, Nuri," Cosmo told her.

"Brain-E, can you fix the Dragster?" Nuri said into her communicator. "I've got to help Cosmo take Junkjet down."

Brain-E's lights flashed from the Dragster's cockpit. "Negative, Miss Nuri. There are too many repairs needed."

Cosmo heard the roar of jet engines overhead and looked up to see Junkjet flying towards a factory space dock where massive asteroid-mining vessels were being built. The alien fired at them with the thermal blaster, melting a line of mechanical cranes. Panicked factory-bots retreated into the spacecraft hangars, closing their big metal doors.

"I will destroy this place!" Junkjet roared, obliterating a transporter with the gamma vaporizer, then destroying a cargo holder and docking bay with a round of photon torpedoes.

Cosmo and Nuri dived for cover beneath a crane as shrapnel from the vessels rained down. *I must stop the invader*, Cosmo thought. He gathered his strength and spoke into the helmet's sensor: "SCAN!" Images of aliens appeared on the visor's digital display: a whip-tongued scorpol . . . a razor-winged wikkon . . . a dagger-toothed mortua . . . He saw an image of a bendy alien with long rope-like arms.

ALIEN: ELASTRON
SPECIES: RUBBEROID
ORIGIN: PLANET BUSE
HEIGHT: VARIABLE
WEIGHT: 100 KILOGRAMS
FEATURE: ELASTIC LIMBS

With elastic limbs I could reach up and pull Junkjet out of the air, Cosmo thought. "MUTATE!"

CHAPTER EIGHT

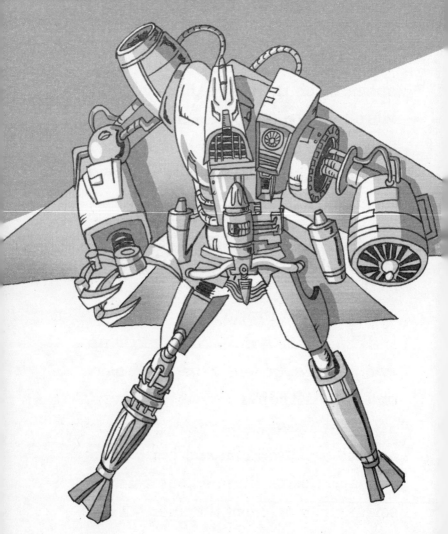

ELASTIC FANTASTIC

Cosmo's Quantum Mutation Suit flickered with blue light and his body tingled, his molecules mutating into those of Elastron. His bones softened and stretched, his arms uncoiling like elastic. *Cool*, he thought, extending his rubbery limbs.

Junkjet zoomed low over the spaceship assembly platform on another bombing run, and Cosmo whipped out his arms, seizing hold of one of the alien's wings.

Junkjet turned to see what had gripped him. Spotting Elastron, he roared: "Hands off me!"

A smile stretched across Cosmo's rubbery face and he yanked hard, pulling Junkjet down towards the factory platform. The invader hit the deck, and engine parts broke off his body. Smoke spewed from one of his jets, and the Dragster's photon cannons broke loose and rolled across the ground. Black oil pooled around him.

"You're finished, Junkjet," Cosmo called, striding over on his bendy legs.

"Never!"

Junkjet staggered to his feet again, and fired his gamma vaporizer, but Cosmo bent his stretchy body to avoid the red rays. A cargo ship and a moon buggy behind him immediately turned to dust. "Missed me!" Cosmo jeered.

Junkjet revved his engines. "I won't miss next time!" And he took off again, circling high overhead.

This flying freak's not a problem for Elastron, Cosmo thought. He made a loop with his arm, and this time swung it at Junkjet like a lasso. It looped around the invader, and he pulled hard, yanking it tight.

"Let go of me!" Junkjet bellowed, trying to prise off Cosmo's elastic hold. But the rubbery arm merely stretched when he pulled it.

"You're going nowhere, Junkjet," Cosmo yelled.

"Wanna bet?"

With Cosmo holding him, Junkjet accelerated, flying around a crane, stretching Cosmo's arms. Then he doubled back, looping and turning. Cosmo realized too late that the invader was tying his arms in a knot!

He let go, trying to ping his arms back, but they were tied to the crane. He was stuck!

The alien glared down at Cosmo, aiming his gamma vaporizer, and

laughed. "I've got you now, boy!"

Cosmo braced himself, preparing to be vaporized.

"Get away, Flunkjet!" Cosmo heard. It was Brain-E's voice. The brave little brainbot was coming to help, using the copter blade attachment from the Dragster's kit shelf. It whizzed up to Junkjet's eye-socket and tugged at a cable, causing one of his eye-lights to spark and go out.

"Aaargh!" Junkjet roared.

"Nice work, Brain-E!" Cosmo yelled.

But he spoke too soon; Junkjet blasted his jets, sending the brainbot tumbling away, crashing onto the deck.

The alien turned back to face Cosmo, who was still tied up, when a roar of engines sounded from nearby. A Starflight rocketship was firing up, tilting on its hydraulic launch pad, aiming straight for Junkjet. Sitting in its cockpit was Nuri! It blasted off, flames shooting out of its rockets, and smashed into the invader, knocking him aside. The alien went tumbling across the platform, smashing straight through the wall of a hangar.

"Thanks, Nuri," Cosmo called, seeing her veer away and regain control as she circled the factory. "RESET," he said, and his knotted arms untied as he turned back into a boy wearing the Quantum Mutation Suit.

He ran to the hangar and peered inside to where Junkjet had crashed. The hangar housed dozens of Starflight's latest high-performance sports spacecraft, and Junkjet lay on the ground, eyeing them eagerly.

The invader's engine spluttered as he staggered to his feet, looking dented and mangled. His wings had snapped off, and from his jets came a clattering sound as if something had broken inside.

"Give up, Junkjet!' Cosmo called, his voice echoing inside the hangar.

"You fool, Earthboy!" the invader bellowed, reaching for the gleaming new sports spacecraft all around him. "There are enough ship parts in here to make me invincible. Now you'll never stop me!" He strode to a TOK50 Starstreaker and ripped out its neutron engine, then tore the turbo-turbinator off a TUFF 12.6. He attached each of the gleaming new engines to his own body and wrenched a wing from a sleek red CAPE V-Force speed-racer to replace his broken one. Plucking a high-powered headlight from

a MINKY-J, he fitted it into his broken eye-socket. His metallicon flesh meshed with all the different machine parts, absorbing them into his body. He was growing stronger all the time. "I feel goooood!" he roared, and flew out over Cosmo, blasting open the hangar roof.

With a whoosh from his new neutron engines he shot up into the air, doing a loop-the-loop, then swooped down and prised the roof off another hangar housing hundreds of new spaceships ready to be shipped throughout the galaxy. "DESTROY!" he roared.

Nuri, still circling in the rocketship, shot after him and tried to smash him aside again, but this time Junkjet turned the gamma vaporizer on her and fired. A hatch opened in the rocketship's cockpit and Nuri ejected just as the gamma ray hit and the ship disintegrated.

One last try, Cosmo thought. "SCAN,"

he said into the sensor of the Quantum Mutation Suit. On the visor's display, images of aliens appeared once again. He spotted an alien made entirely from dust.

ALIEN: DUST STORM
SPECIES: DRAXIAN
ORIGIN: THE DESERTS OF NIXL
HEIGHT: VARIABLE
WEIGHT: VARIABLE
FEATURE: AMORPHOUS BODY

Cosmo had an idea. *Let's see how Junkjet survives a dust storm!* he said to himself. "MUTATE."

CHAPTER NINE

IN PIECES

Cosmo's body began changing for a third time as his molecules mutated into those of Dust Storm. He felt the moisture leaving his flesh; he was drying out and breaking into chunks. Then each chunk disintegrated into dust. *This feels . . . unusual*, he thought, now in tiny pieces but still able to sense and move.

Junkjet fired flames from the thermal blaster and rays from the gamma vaporizer, destroying the ships in the hangar: microjets, cargo transporters, space ploughs, sunships and drones.

Cosmo's dust body swirled up from the ground like a phantom, a hollow mouth forming. "That's enough, metalhead!" he called, sweeping after the invader. "Bad weather coming your way!'

Junkjet saw Cosmo and fired a wave of gamma rays at him, but as Dust Storm,

Cosmo merely swirled out of the way.

"You'll have to try better than that," he said defiantly.

Frustrated, Junkjet fired his thermal blaster, but it had no effect either; Cosmo simply dispersed his dust body to dodge the flames, then re-formed once they'd passed.

"Run out of ideas yet?" Cosmo called.

Junkjet powered his jets and shot towards Cosmo, his sharp metal claw

outstretched. But as Dust Storm, Cosmo was ungrippable. His tiny dust particles flew into Junkjet's engines, clogging the mechanical parts.

From inside Junkjet came a *BANG!* like an engine backfiring, and the invader stalled in mid-air. Unable to repower, he plummeted, roaring as he fell, and crashed to the ground with a *CRUNCH!*

As Dust Storm, Cosmo flew out of Junkjet and re-formed, phantom-like, his dust particles gathering together. He gave the command, "RESET," then felt his body tingle as he mutated back into a boy.

"Get away!" the invader spluttered angrily. He lay broken on the ground, dirty oil leaking from his engines, black smoke rising from his thrusters.

"It's time you left this galaxy, Junkjet." He summoned the power inside him, and the Quantum Mutation Suit glowed. Power surged from Cosmo's core to his fingertips, and his gloved hand tingled and flashed as a sword of energy extended from it like lightning. "The power of the universe is in me!" he said, raising the power sword and plunging it into the invader.

Junkjet roared: "NOOOOOO!"

Cosmo felt every molecule in his body shudder and shake as his power battled

against Junkjet's. The alien's body began to buckle, and silver liquid oozed from cracks in his bodywork as his living metallicon flesh melted. His engines gave one last sputter, then, with a *BOOM!* he exploded into smoke and flames.

Cosmo was sent flying by the force of the blast, his ears ringing and his visor smeared with soot. He sat up, wiping it away with his gloved hand, and saw Nuri rushing over. "Cosmo, you did it! You defeated Junkjet!"

"Well done, Master Cosmo," Brain-E said, flying awkwardly to join them, its copter blade attachment bent and buckled. "Dust Storm was a very clever transformation indeed."

Cosmo surveyed the damage: battered spaceships lay all around. "Junkjet's made quite a mess," he said.

"Starflight's factory-bots will soon have it cleared up," Brain-E replied.

All across the space platform, factory-bots were already emerging from hangars and hiding places to begin the task of repairing the damage.

Cosmo glanced at the Dragster. It had claw marks down its hull and its photon cannons were lying on the ground. "Brain-E, do you think Starflight's factory-bots would help get the Dragster up and running again?"

"An excellent idea," Brain-E replied. "I will ask them straight away."

Nuri helped Cosmo to his feet. "And you and I can check out the sports craft in the hangars while we're waiting," she said. "They look awesome."

"I'd like that, Nuri," Cosmo replied. "Though there's only one ship for me." And he gestured to the Dragster, smiling, relieved to have succeeded in his mission.

CHAPTER TEN

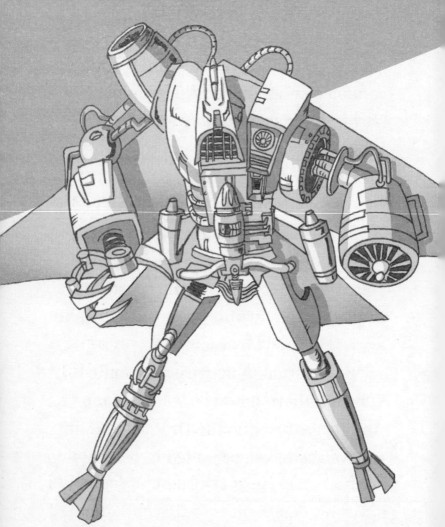

THREE MORE TO COME

Back on the battleship *Oblivion*, the five-headed outlaw Kaos was in the cargo hold making adjustments to an electronic circuit board, soldering components onto it.

A metallicon alien with massive drill-arms and a head caged in metal bars stood watching him. "Is that for me, sir?"

"Yes, Minox, these are your invasion instructions," Kaos's third head replied. "I have encoded them onto this circuit board.

It is quite the best invasion plan so far."

"I don't know why you're wasting your time with that," Kaos's second head said to his third. "When my plan for Junkjet succeeds, G-Watch and the galaxy will surrender. There won't be any need to send in another invader."

But just then a nervous *"Eeek! Eeek!"* sounded from the doorway. Kaos looked down and saw Wugrat coming in.

"What is it, Wugrat?"

"Eeeeeeek!" Wugrat squeaked loudly.

"What do you mean, Junkjet's failed!"

"Eeek, eek, eek!"

"Junkjet's ocular camera is down? His vital signs are at zero?"

"Eek!"

The colour drained from Kaos's second head as he realised what had happened. The other four stared at him with contempt.

"Noooooooooo!" the second head cried.

"Junkjet's been defeated by that blasted Earthling boy!"

"So now it's time for *my* plan," Kaos's third head said with relish. He glanced at Minox, the drill-armed metallicon. "Minox, I'm sending you into the galaxy!"

"Yes, Master," the huge alien replied.

Kaos prised open a metal panel on the alien's chest, revealing cabling and silver metallicon flesh. He slotted in the circuit board containing the alien's invasion plan, and Minox's innards absorbed it like a fresh bodypart, assimilating it into his nervous system.

"Now, are you ready to destroy?" Kaos's third head asked him.

"Yes, Master!" the alien replied.

"Then let's do this!" Kaos fetched a crystal navicom transporter from a box by the doorway, turned its outer ring to set the co-ordinates, then fastened it to Minox. "Minox, do not fail me," he said.

The alien strode to the middle of the hold and the roof opened. He revved his drill-arms, spinning them wildly. "I will destroy-y-y-y!"

The navicom started to flash and a blue light radiated from it. With a *whoosh*, Minox shot out into space.

"Power is restored," Brain-E radioed from the Dragster. "It's ready to fly now."

"We're on our way," Cosmo replied into his helmet's mic, returning with Nuri from checking out the sports craft. They passed by the robots that had been repairing the Dragster, then climbed aboard. Cosmo sat in the pilot's seat as Brain-E flicked a sequence of switches on the control desk, rebooting the flight systems. He heard the soft hum of the engines.

"All systems are go," the brainbot said.

Relieved that the Dragster was fixed after its battle with Junkjet, Cosmo patted the control desk. "Good to have you back, old friend."

Nuri typed a code into the Dragster's communications console, and the face of G1, Chief of G-Watch, appeared on its monitor. "Hi, G1," she said. "Starflight is safe. Junkjet is history."

The silver-eyed Chief smiled.

"Cosmo was ace," Nuri added. "He mutated into Dust Storm and clogged Junkjet's engines."

"Excellent thinking, Cosmo. You are certainly living up to your rank of Agent Supreme," G1 replied. "Thanks to you, Starflight will continue to manufacture the galaxy's finest spaceships."

"It was a team effort, Chief," Cosmo replied. "And all in the line of duty."

G1's green face took on a serious expression. "Listen up," he said. "Junkjet may be defeated, but a third alien has already been dispatched from the Wrecking Zone. Our scanners identify it as the metallicon Minox, and it's heading for a site of great scientific importance for our galaxy: Planet Balaz in the Alpha Quadrant. You must go after it."

"We're on our way, G1," Cosmo said. "Over and out." He switched off the monitor and called out of the exit door to the factory-bots. "Thanks for your help, but we've got to go now."

The Starflight factory-bots moved away from the Dragster and waved as the cockpit door slid shut.

Cosmo powered up the thrusters. "OK, team, let's go get Minox!" he said, and with a roar the Dragster blasted off into space.

Join Cosmo on his next **ALIEN INVADERS**
mission. He must face - and defeat

MINOX
THE PLANET DRILLER

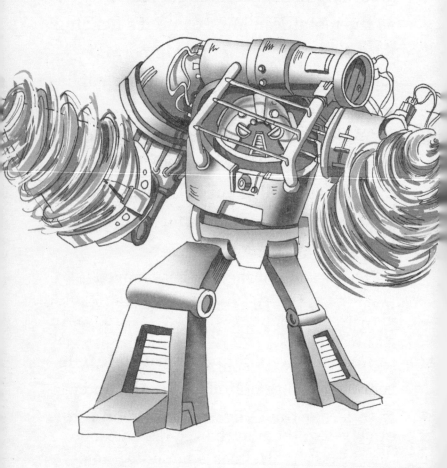

INVADER ALERT!

Underground on Planet Balaz, Professor Vorp crawled down a narrow tunnel on his pincers and knees, shining his head torch towards a large cavern up ahead.

"We're almost there, R6," he said, glancing back at the lights of an explorobot walking behind on suckered legs. "Keep up."

"Coming, Professor," R6 replied in its computerized voice.

Professor Vorp reached the cavern and stood up, stretching his long Diluvian arms. He glanced at the ceiling and walls, his head torch illuminating red mosses, furry lichen, insects, molluscs and even scurrying reptiles. "R6, log our co-ordinates and let's begin recording these plants and creatures."

The robot whirred. "Investigation point nine. Depth twenty-two metres," it relayed. A sampling tube extended from a tank on its back and, with short sucking sounds, it hoovered up a sample of each insect species.

"That's it, R6," Professor Vorp said. "We can observe them in the zoo-lab back on the spaceship." He took a handheld holo-cam from his pocket and snapped holographs of fork-tailed lizards that were scuttling across the walls. "The Institute will be amazed at our findings."

Professor Vorp and his explorobot, R6, were on an expedition to Planet Balaz for the Galactic Institute of New Alien Life as part of an ongoing study to document the planet's unique underground life forms.

At the back of the cavern, the professor noticed a wide tunnel sloping steeply away. Curious, he shone his torch down it to another chamber below that was overgrown with fleshy plants the likes of which he'd never seen before. Each had large mouth-like pods writhing on long twisted stalks. One pod snapped at a fork-tailed lizard and gobbled it down whole.

"R6, there's a new species of carnivorous plant down here," the professor called, edging down the sloping tunnel to get a better view. He stopped short of the plants and, gripping a rock with one pincer to stop himself falling into them, reached out his holo-cam to take a few holographs. *Click! Click! Click!*

"Be careful, Professor," R6 called from the top of the slope.

"I'm just taking a few shots," Professor Vorp replied. *Click! Click! Click!*

BOOOOM! Suddenly there came a deafening sound from above, and the walls and ceiling shuddered. The professor lost his grip and almost tumbled down the slope, dropping his holo-cam as he steadied himself. He saw it fall among the plants below where it was snapped up and chomped.

"What was that, R6?" the professor called, looking back to the upper cavern.

But his words were drowned out by the sound of a roaring engine. Slabs and boulders started falling from above, knocking R6 to the floor. Professor Vorp watched, horrified, as a monstrous alien with huge spinning drill-arms tore through the cavern's roof, eyes blazing in a caged metal skull.

The professor lurched back in shock and, losing his grip, tumbled into the flesh-eating plants below.

As a large plant pod gripped him, he heard the huge alien roar. "I am Minox, and I am programmed to DRILL!"

CHAPTER ONE
A BARREN PLANET?

"OK, Cosmo, try this," Agent Nuri said. "Ten, nine, eight, seven, *verva, vox—*"

"*Verva? Vox?* No, I'm still not hearing you right, Nuri," Cosmo replied. "Can you take over while I sort this out?"

Nuri took control of the Dragster 7000 spaceship from the co-pilot's seat, and Cosmo removed his space helmet, tilted his head to one side and tapped it twice.

From the control desk, the ship's brainbot, Brain-E, bleeped. "Let me help you, Master Cosmo," it said, climbing onto Cosmo's shoulder and extending a pincer probe towards his ear. "Hold still."

Cosmo felt the cold metal probe extending into his skull. Then it retracted, pulling out a wriggling orange worm.

"Just as I suspected – your wordsworm has got itself in a twist," Brain-E said, pointing to a knot in the worm's middle. "No wonder it's making mistakes."

Wordsworms were standard kit for galactic travellers, placed inside the ear to translate between the millions of languages spoken in the galaxy. Four times in the last hour, Cosmo's worm had mistranslated words, causing confusion between him and his Etrusian co-pilot, Agent Nuri.

Cosmo unknotted the worm, wiped some earwax off it, then popped it back into his ear, feeling it wriggle deep inside again.

"Is it working OK now?" Nuri asked.

Cosmo understood her clearly this time. "It seems to be," he said, replacing his helmet. "Co-ordinates please."

"Planet Balaz is about 150,000 Earth kilometres southwest of here in the Alpha Quadrant," Nuri said.

"Roger that," Cosmo replied, taking back control of the ship and powering it past a diamond-shaped star system. "OK, let's go save the galaxy."

Cosmo, Nuri and Brain-E were on a mission for the galactic security force G-Watch to battle five alien invaders under the command of the outlaw Kaos. So far Cosmo had defeated two of them: Krush, the iron giant, and Junkjet, the flying menace. Now he was off to Planet Balaz to face the third, identified by G-Watch scanners as Minox.

"What do we know about this invader, Brain-E?" Cosmo asked.

"Minox is evolved from wrecked asteroid-mining vessels, with drill-arms able to pierce solid rock."

"Solid rock!"

"Planet Balaz straight ahead," Nuri said, looking up from the navigation console.

Cosmo tried to stay brave as their destination came into view: an isolated black planet. Flying into its atmosphere, he set the spacescreen to zoom mode; the planet's surface appeared desolate and barren. "Why would Kaos send an invader to this place? There's nothing here," he said.

"I suspect because Balaz is a Great Wonder of the galaxy," Brain-E explained. "Technically it is not a planet at all, but the largest living organism in existence."

"Living organism?" Cosmo said, amazed.

"Yes. In recent times Balaz has been observed by scientists to be growing. Investigations have revealed it to be a huge spherical creature and host to all kinds of other life forms that live within it."

Cosmo flew the Dragster lower, shining the searchlights onto Balaz's cracked surface. "So I'm looking at its skin?"

"That's right, Master Cosmo."

"Get ready to land," Nuri interrupted. "G-Watch scanners indicate Minox beamed in just a few kilometres east of here."

It's crunch time, Cosmo thought, checking Balaz's environment and preparing to land:

PLENTIFUL OXYGEN . . . TEMPERATURE TEN DEGREES CENTIGRADE . . . GRAVITY NORMAL

Cosmo felt his courage welling, and his spacesuit, the Quantum Mutation Suit, started to glow.

Below, a crater came into view where Balaz's skin had been opened up by some kind of large impact. "This must be where Minox struck," Cosmo said, taking the Dragster lower. There was no sign of the invader now – just a space research ship nearby, and a small robot clambering from the rubble.

Brain-E bleeped in alarm. "According to my databank, a Professor Vorp of the Galactic Institute of New Alien Life is currently exploring Balaz. That robot must be his companion explorobot."

"So where's the professor now?" Cosmo

asked, scanning the rubble. The Dragster touched down and he opened its cockpit door and ran to the crater. He and Nuri scrambled down to the explorobot and together pulled it out, setting it back on its suckered feet.

"Monster crashed down and drilled underground," the explorobot said. "Professor Vorp trapped. Investigation point nine. Depth twenty-two metres."

"He must be beneath this lot," Nuri said, gesturing to the mass of rubble and rocks in the crater. "We'll need to clear a way through." But the rocks looked heavy, and moving them would be slow work.

"Brain-E, please could you check this explorobot is OK," Cosmo asked, and as Nuri began removing rubble from the crater, searching for Professor Vorp, he looked for a quicker way down, fearing for the professor if Minox was down there too. Around the crater, in Balaz's crust, he noticed cracks wide enough for a person to fit through, like vertical shafts into the planet. "Nuri, keep clearing. I'm going to try another way."

Cosmo squeezed down into a shaft at

the crater's edge, lowering himself through the planet's crust. Down he climbed through darkness, dropping into a tunnel just big enough to crawl along on his elbows and knees. He unclipped his plasma torch from his utility belt and switched it on, sending fork-tailed lizards scuttling from its light. The tunnel led to an underground chamber full of tall writhing plants with gnashing mouth-like pods. Cosmo gasped, seeing a space boot lying on the ground among them. "Professor Vorp, are you in here?" he called.

**Find out what happens in
MINOX – THE PLANET DRILLER . . .**